BEACH SCHOOL

WHAT FEELS BEST?

by Anita Harper
illustrated by Susan Hellard

G.P. Putnam's Sons · New York

When Grandma gave me some candy
for my birthday, I ate it all myself . . .

But I didn't feel good.

And when Dad gave me a bike,
I wouldn't let anyone else ride it.

That didn't feel good either.

If I'm feeling angry or upset,
I go off by myself.

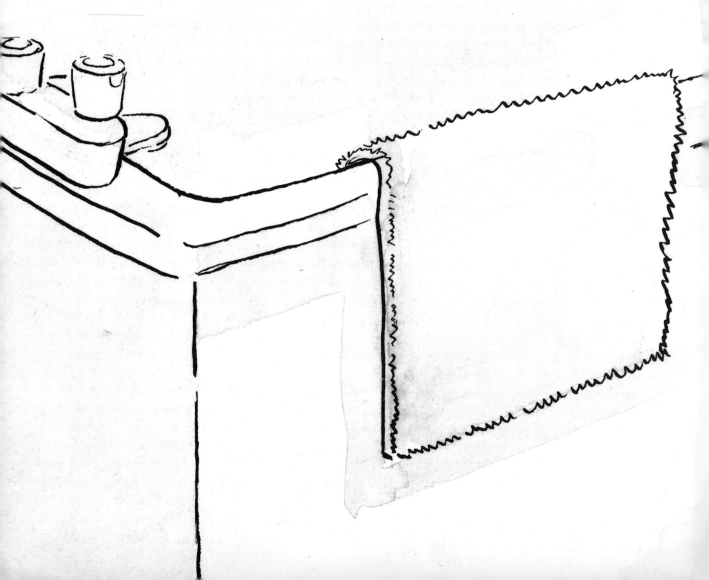

But it doesn't feel right.

And once my friend needed some help,
but I wouldn't give her any.

I didn't feel good about that.

The day I decided to build a treehouse
I didn't tell anyone.

BEACH SCHOOL

But I really needed some help.

After a while I began to feel lonely.

So when Mom made me a cake,
I asked my friends to share it.

That felt better.

And when my teacher gave me a special job,
I let my friends help.

That felt good.

The day I learned a new jump,
I showed my brother how to do it to

We had fun.

The last time I felt sad,
I told someone.

That helped.

When I found out about the stars and planets,
I told everyone.

That really felt good.

Sharing something together —
that feels best!